THE BOOK OF AUSTRALIAN NURSERY RHYME
by Bindi–Bindi
Illustrated by Heather Blackstock

Published by
BINDI–BINDI PUBLISHING
63 HAMLYN ROAD
OAKEY, QLD. 4401
PHONE/FAX. (07) 4691 2317
First Printing 1999

Disclaimer: Any names used in these Nursery Rhymes have
no reference to any person living or dead.

Copyright © Bindi-Bindi 1999
ISBN-0-646-36312-3

Printed in Australia by
Fergies
Phone: (07) 3268 2700

ALL POSTAL PAYMENTS TO: OAKEY ADDRESS
ALL ORDERS TO: (07) 4691 2317 (Phone or Fax.)

AUXILIARY CONTACT ONLY: 10 PARKVIEW CRES.
YAMBA, NSW, 2464
PHONE/FAX. (02) 6646 8364

Author's Note

Ever since European settlement in Australia, our children have been raised on an assortment of Nursery Rhyme originating in the Northern Hemisphere. We at Bindi-Bindi thought a change was long overdue.

While the concept of *The Book of Australian Nursery Rhyme* had been thought about, nothing positive happened until the 1980's when a considerable amount of material was produced. However the whole thing did not come together until early 1999, when we were ready to go to print.

Where possible, the Rhymes have been set in <u>early 20th Century</u> to give children a taste of yesteryear Australia. The five page Glossary at the back of the book gives additional information to share with our little ones as they grow.

It is our sincere hope that this collection of original Australian Nursery Rhyme, so beautifully illustrated, will give generations of reading pleasure to children of Australia and overseas.

BINDI-BINDI PUBLISHING

About the Artist

Heather Blackstock, who currently resides on Queenland's Gold Coast, grew up in the Dorrigo region of New South Wales, where she began to develop a love for Australian Flora and Fauna.

After winning a prize for her first exhibit, Heather went on to win many art awards, and her work is now represented in private and city collections in Australia and Overseas.

From 1986 to 1996, Heather taught Art at the T.A.F.E. College on the Gold Coast, before graduating in Creative Arts at Griffith University in 1996.

A message to each child

**We hope you will enjoy this book of rhyme,
and we hope you will read it from time to time.
We trust you will learn from these pages true,
and you'll make real friends with our animal crew.
So whenever you open this picture-book,
and at each new animal you take a look,
there's and important message for us to find....
TO ENJOY THESE CREATURES, WE MUST BE KIND.**

Contents

THIS BOOK BELONGS
TO:

Seeing Australia

If you want to cross the Nullarbor,
it's best to go by train.
If you want to see Ayers Rock,
it's best to go by plane.
And if to see the Barrier Reef,
you have to go by boat.

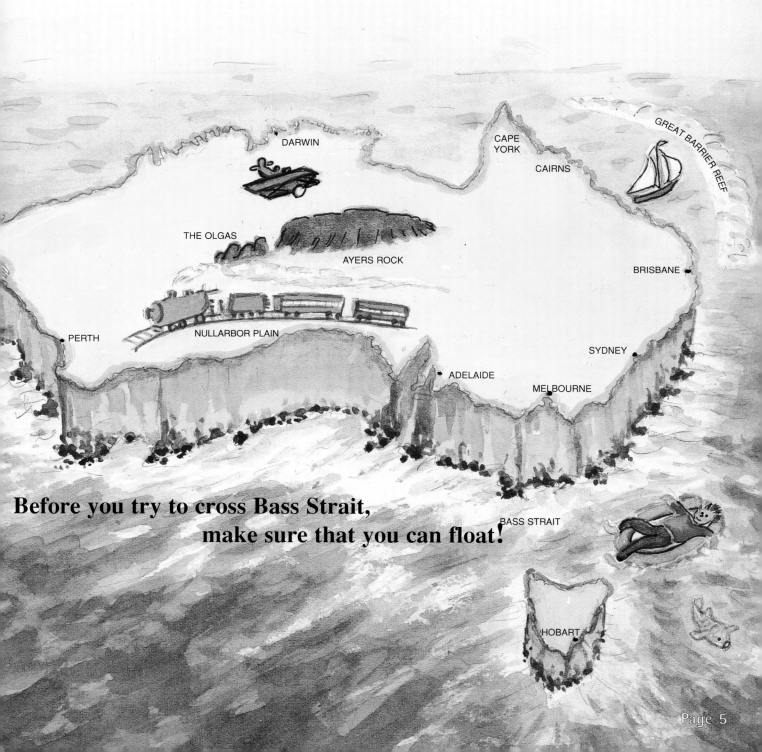

Before you try to cross Bass Strait,
make sure that you can float!

Koala In The Tree

Can you see koala,
    sitting in the tree?
He likes yummy gumtips
    for brekky, lunch and tea.

The Platypus

Have you seen our Platypus?
  He's nothing like this fluffy puss.
He swims under water,
  has little webbed feet,
Bill like a duck,
  I think he's so neat.

Two Black Crows

Out in the west where the country's dry,
two black Crows went flying by,
with beady eyes and clothes so dark,
all they said was, "Ark! Ark! Ark!"

Would you like to be a Crow,
flying where you want to go?
It would be, such a lark,
Who could see you after dark?

A Pelican A'Sailing

I saw a Pelican A'sailing,
A'sailing out to sea.
He used his feet for paddles,
he flapped his wings with glee.

He said "I'll sail the ocean wide,
I'll sail on every sea,
I won't return to Sydney town
until I'm Twenty Three!"

Hoppy the Kangaroo

Hop! hop! hop! goes the Kangaroo
Hop! hop! hop! right to the Zoo.
It will take him quite a while
from here to there,
it's about one mile.

Wally Wombat

Wally Wombat is so fat,
he's twice as big as
our pussy cat.

He sleeps all day
and half the night

and then some more
if the moon is bright.

Off To Sea

I had a Kookaburra,

      but nothing would he cook,

I had a little puppy-dog,

      who used to chase our chook,

I had a Willy Wagtail,

      who would not wag his tail,

So I sent them off to sea

      in a boat that had no sail.

Off To Sea (2)

But after just a little while,
        I started feeling sad,
to send my little friends to sea,
        was something very bad,
so I went and brought them home again,
        and promised them that day,
that I would always care for them,
        at home with me they'd stay.

Willy Wagtail

Willy Wagtail hops along,
        but doesn't seem to have a song,
His tail sticks up, his wings go flap,
        he's such a cheeky little chap.

His suit is black, his tie is white,
        all his feathers are shiny bright,

But try to catch him
        in your net,
And lots of air
        is all you'll get.

Mr Emu

Here comes Emu standing tall,
Great big feet so he can't fall,
Big round eyes that blink and stare,
He looks down on Mr Hare.

Danny Dingo

Danny Dingo is like a dog,
sitting there
beside that log.
But he's not a puppy
to take home,
'cause o'r the hills
he likes to roam.

Big Bad Crocodile

Crocodile is mean and long
     Big sharp teeth, and very strong.
Basking all day in the sun.
     If he sees you, Run! Run! Run!

Butcher Bird

Butcher Bird! O Butcher Bird,
sweetest call I've ever heard,
when I hear your lovely song,
I wish that I could sing along.

<u>Mrs Magpie</u>

Mrs Magpie will protect her nest,
to many people she is a pest.
Just when you think it's safe to stay,
she'll swoop and peck you on your way.
So if you're passing by her nest,
do not tarry! do not rest!
To Mrs Magpie, you're the pest,
you're just one more unwelcome guest.

Aussie Echidna

Why its Aussie Echidna, not Porcupine!
And may I ask just where you dine?
And when you sit, do you feel a quill
When you go to bed, are your spines
out still?

You look so smart in your spikey coat
And it has been said, you can swim and float?
But should you wander near my shack
Don't ask me to scratch your back!

Little Gecko

BONDI 1920

See the lizard on the wall
Has sticky feet so he can't fall
Little Gecko is his name
Catching insets is his game.

<u>Kookaburra</u>

Kookaburra is happy and gay.
     He wakes us at the break of day
With his Kook! Kook! Kook!
     and his Kaa! Kaa! Kaa!
Laughing, Laughing from afar
     Let's join in with a Ho! Ho! Ho!
        Let's join in with a Ha! Ha! Ha!

The White Cockatoo

Cockatoo! O Cockatoo!
　　What is it you like to do?
"I like to eat corn,
　　and I like to eat seed.
When I get hungry,
　　that's what I need!"

Benny Bunny

Benny Bunny likes his honey,
 Says it makes him feel quite funny.
But when he spreads it very thick,
 It makes poor Benny feel quite sick.

Harold Hare

Say hello to Harold Hare,
He feeds all day on local fare,
Has lots of brothers and sisters too,
Uncles and Aunts, yes quite a few.
They pop up here, they pop up there,
There's Bunny Rabbits everywhere.

Wise Old Owl

Wise Old Owl up in the tree
has big round eyes
that stare at me.
Then he blinks
and flies away
Hoot! Hoot! Hoot!
is all he'll say.

My Little Parrot

I have a little Parrot
        that likes to talk to me.
He sits upon my shoulder
        and then upon my knee.
If I ask him nicely,
        he will stay to tea.
Eating yummy biscuits
        one, two, three.

My Woolly Lamb

Waddle goes the duck,
      Waggle goes the geese.
I have a woolly lamb,
      that has a golden fleece.

Once a year I shear him
      to make a woolly coat.
But then he gets so cranky,
      he starts to chase the goat.

Tassie Devil

Tassie Devil, although quite small,
is most unfriendly, I do recall,
he's always in a grumpy mood,
growls and snarles, won't share his food.
Has very bad manners, and looks so wild,
he acts just like a naughty child,
so my advice, and I think it's true,
it's best to meet him at the zoo!

The Pink and Grey Galah

Hear the Pink and Grey Galah?
He's calling to us from afar
    He's calling with his squeaky whistle
    Always looking for a thistle.

Then he lands upon a branch,
    And starts to do his little dance,
        With head awry and crest up high
        He's showing off 'cause he can fly.

Tommy Turtle

Tommy Turtle by the brook
Loves to read his story book.
He turns the pages two by two
with pretty pictures,
quite a few.

But if you start to make a din
he will pull his head right in.

Mrs Possum

Don't call me possum
I'm Mrs Possum
See, in this gumtree
among the blossom.

Silver-grey brushtail
just a touch of black
Can you see my baby
clinging to my back?

I love to eat fruit,
and I love to taste cheese,
if I come to visit,
will you give me some, please?

Tiny Tadpole

Tadpole! Tadpole! in the pool,
you're too young to go to school,
swimming by that mossy log,
one day soon you'll be a frog.

Nellie Numbat

Nellie Numbat with pointed nose
  on a termite nest, just loves to pose
With striped fur coat and bushy tail
She's looking at the moon so pale.

So should you pass by that hollow log
and by the way, don't bring the dog.
  for in that log is a grassy nest
    with three baby numbats,
      taking their rest.

Swagman Bill

Swagman Bill came down the hill,
to the creek, his billy to fill,
with old dog Bluey at his heel,
it's tea and damper for their meal.

Can You?

Can you "Hullabaloo" like a Cockatoo?

Can you hop "True Blue" like a Kangaroo?

Can you crawl awhile like a Crocodile?

Can you run and skip for half a mile?

Can you catch a rat like our Tabby Cat?

Can you chase a hen like a Fairy Wren?

Can you frill your gizzard like a Frilly Lizard?

Can you scare a cat like a Bent-Wing Bat?

Can you shake your tail just like a Quail?

Can you cry and howl like a Mallee Fowl?

Can you to and fro like an old Black Crow?

Can you jump a log like a Green-Tree Frog?

Bush Flies

Those flies are flying all around,
I wish they'd go away,
So I can eat my lunch in peace,
then I can go and play.
I have some corks upon my hat,
a swatter in my hand
I'm watching very closely,
to see where next they'll land

they walk around my
mouth and nose
they tramp across my face
and never do they wipe their feet
they are a real disgrace.

Kenny's Pet

Kenny Hoad from down the road
Tied a string around the neck of a toad

"I'll take you home to be my pet
and in no time at all
you'll be glad we met."

TOAD ROAD

BAKER

BLACKSMITH

Kenny's Pet (2)

"I'll feed you icecream and lollies too,
We'll eat sweet biscuits, yes quite a few,
And when you're tired, and the day is through,
I'll make you a bed in my daddy's shoe."

Fat Tom

There was a young man his
name was Tom
He put jam and cream
on every scone.

He loved his cakes
and biscuits too,

But not a door could he get through.

<u>Billy Bock</u>

There was a little boy,
    His name was Billy Bock
He took his daddy's hammer,
    He said he'd fix the clock.

He hit it on the front side
He hit it on the back

But when he tried to wind it up
It would not go Tick! Tock!

Herbert Hathaway

Little Herbert Hathaway
his teeth
he would not clean,
so after
ten and twenty days
they started
turning green,
they even
started falling out
they fell
upon the floor,

So Herbert's mummy
took the broom
And swept them out the
door.

Herbert Hathaway (2)

So do you clean
your teeth at night,
before you go to bed?
And after eating breakfast,
just like your mummy said?
Yes! If you're wise
you'll clean them
morning noon and nights.
And unlike Herbert Hathaway
you'll keep your pearly whites.

Little Bobby Bottomly

Little Bobby Bottomly would never wash his face.
His ears and neck were dirty, it was a real disgrace.
He hated soap and water, he would not touch a towel,
When bath time came around each day,
He let out such a howl.
But after quite a little while
the dirt got very thick,
He began to feel so awful,
he said he felt quite sick.
So he rushed off to the bathroom,
and started in to scrub,
with lots of soapy water
filling up the bathroom tub.

Bobby Bottomly (2)

He began to feel much better,
And promised her that day,
   When mummy called him for his bath
      He'd come in right away.
So when your mummy calls you,
   "Come in now from your play,"
Remember Bobby Bottomly
      And hurry to obey.

At the Farm

We're off to visit Gran and Pa,
Who have a little farm,
I'm getting so excited,
Mummy says I must be calm,
Grandma will be waiting,
To give us all a hug,
And when we go to bed at night,
We'll be so warm and snug.

At the Farm - (2)

But tomorrow there'll be much to do,
the cows to milk
and the horse to shoe

Chickens to feed,
and the hay to bale.
A pig to get ready
for the country sale.

And while we're all toiling
in the yard,
Gran's in her kitchen
working hard,
baking lots of cakes and biscuits too,
and a hearty lunch for her hungry crew.

Then after lunch there'll be games to play,
you can be sure we'll enjoy our stay,
but when it's time to say goodbye,
we'll be quite sad, how the time did fly.

Glossary

Page 5 **SEEING AUSTRALIA** The Nullarbor (treeless plain). This vast low plateau, located inland from the Great Australian Bight and measuring about 700km long by 400km wide, is dissected by the Western Australian and South Australian border. It is believed that the limestone base is so porous, that the rainfall disappears too quickly for trees to become established. The main East-West Highway runs well to the South of the true Nullarbor.

AYERS ROCK (Aboriginal ULURU) is another natural wonder. This massive sandstone monolith rising 350 meters out of the flat landscape and submerged 2000 meters into the earth, is the largest stone in the world. It is almost 10km around the base, and thousands of tourists enjoy the spectacle every year. While the Rock can be climbed by those with reasonable fitness, there has been loss of life over the years.

THE OLGAS (Aboriginal KATA TJUTA) can be clearly seen from the top of Ayers Rock. Another natural phenomenon, this ancient oddity is not sandstone as is Ayers Rock but is formed of conglomerate. The Olgas consist of a group of beehive-like domes, the tallest being 546 metres, while the total circumference is about 20km.

THE GREAT BARRIER REEF This is the largest coral reef in the world, stretching almost the entire length of Queensland. This magnificent spectacle, with its 250 tropical islands, draws visitors and holiday makers from around the world.

BASS STRAIT This waterway between the island state of Tasmania and the mainland, is quite dangerous to small shipping, and in gales, to larger vessels. The Strait is named after the early English explorer George Bass. On February 5, 1803, Bass departed Sydney on the brig Venus, and was never heard from again.

Page 6 **KOALA IN A TREE** This distinctive Australian bear spends its life high in the trees, feeding on the leaves of certain flavoured Eucalypts including the Red Gum, the Grey Gum and the Blue Gum. Adult males can weigh up to 14kg females up to 11kg. The female is often seen with a baby on her back. Koalas can sleep quite comfortably in the fork of a tree.

GUM TIPS fresh young leaves   **YUMMY** tasty   **TEA** dinner, evening meal   **BREKKY** breakfast

Page 7 **THE PLATYPUS** This unique creature which has confounded the scientific community, can reach the length of 50cm and can weigh 1.5kg. It is timid by nature and usually lives in a burrow along a creek bank. It feeds on water plants and small aquatic life. The female lays eggs like a bird, yet suckles her young when hatched, from milk ducts located on her abdomen. It is common along the East coast of Australia, including Tasmania.

Page 8 **TWO BLACK CROWS** Crows are of the Raven family, a large bird growing to 45cm. Their call is a loud cawing cry, at times ending with a drawn-out gargle. Their black feathers are not well suited to the hot, dry West and more and more seem to be moving to coastal areas. It is a scavenger and can often be seen at the roadside where dead fauna provide a ready meal.

LARK A slang name for a prank or trick.

Page 9 **THE PELICAN** This is a very large seabird, usually found along the coast, can also be found in large numbers on inland waterways, where it goes to breed and raise its young. It uses its bag-like bill to scoop up fish to swallow. This large bird can grow to 1.2 meters with a wingspan of 3.5 meters. This majestic creature can often be seen following working trawlers in the hope of a free meal.

Page 10 **THE KANGAROO** Probably the animal most associated with Australia. It is the largest of this family of grazing animals, ranging down through the Wallabies, Quokkas, Bettongs, Pademelons and smaller. Some main groups are Eastern Grey, Western Grey and Red. Males can grow 2.4 meters tall and weigh 70kg. The female has a distinctive front pouch, concealing four teats, where it suckles a single young for up to six months. The Kangaroos powerful back legs enable it to cover considerable distances quickly in great bounds, using its heavy tail for balance. The Kangaroo is featured with the Emu on the Australian Coat of Arms.

Page 11 **THE WOMBAT** A large burrowing marsupial, weighing up to 40kg. It is shy by nature and is seldom seen in the wild. It is a nocturnal feeder on grasses and roots. The female has a rear opening pouch (unlike the kangaroo/wallaby family) which conceals two teats where the young feed for up to six months. The Common Wombat is found in coastal areas of New South Wales, Victoria and Tasmania. Other lesser known species can be found in isolated areas of South Australia and Queensland.

Page 12 **CHOOK** A slang name for a hen.

Page 14 **WILLY WAGTAIL** This small back and white fantail grows to about 20cm. Its call is a brief twittering. It is viewed affectionately by people generally, and is at home in the suburban garden or on the back of a cow, removing blood sucking ticks.

Page 15 **THE EMU** The largest native Australian bird, resembling the African Ostrich, though smaller, is usually found in outback Australia where it grazes over large areas. Cattle Station owners (ranchers) regard them as pests, as they can break fences and ruin pasture. After the female lays the eggs, it is the male that does the brooding, usually about 8 weeks. It is not uncommon, when travelling through the outback, to see proud parents with 8 to 10 chicks at heel. The Emu shares the Australian Coat of Arms with the Kangaroo.

Page 16 **THE DINGO** A primitive dog, introduced into Australia prior to European settlement. It is an intelligent hunter, about twice the size of the Australian fox and can range in colour from blackish brown to cream and white. Like the rabbit (also introduced) the Dingo has at times reached plague proportions, moving the government to place a bounty on its head. In a further attempt to limit its spread, and to protect the large sheep population, the Government built the longest fence in the world, stretching some 5,500km from Ceduna in South Australia to Dalby in Queensland.

Page 17 **THE CROCODILE** There are two principle species in Australia, the small Freshwater or Johnston River Crocodile, which frequents fresh waterways in Northern Australia, and is easily recognised by its narrow snout. It is harmless to man. Not so the much larger Salt Water Crocodile which can grow to 6 meters and is literally a man-eater. It flourishes in the river systems of Northern Australia and they have even been observed off the coast. The largest salt water crocodile on record, was shot by a woman near Normanton, on the Gulf of Carpentaria in the Northern Territory. It measured 8.5 meters. Throughout Northern Australia, signs are posted near rivers and lagoons, warning of the danger to campers and swimmers. There are several nature parks in Australia where large crocs can be viewed.

Page 18 **THE BUTCHER BIRD** This every common Australian bird, about the size of a pigeon, ranges in colour from black and white to grey and white. It has little fear of man, and can be easily tamed to take food from the hand. Its name derives from its habit of impaling pieces of food or insects on a thorn or sharp twig as a butcher might hang meat on a hook. It has a lovely carolling song that is quite distinctive and mating pairs will often sing in duet.

Page 19 **THE MAGPIE** About twice the size of the Butcher bird, it is in variations of black and white. It also has a beautiful carolling song, but quite different from the Butcher bird. It is fearless in protecting its nest, and this has made it unpopular when it swoops and pecks unsuspecting passersby.

Page 20 **THE ECHIDNA** (Also called the AUSTRALIAN SPINY ANTEATER) <u>E</u> <u>KID</u> <u>NA</u> This small animal which grows to about 45 cm is not to be confused with the larger European Porcupine. The back of the Echidna is covered with fur and many vertical spines. It has a fast moving tongue for licking up termites. As with the platypus, the Echidna lays an egg, which is then retained in a brood-pouch, where the baby, once hatched, can suck up milk exuded from milk glands.

SHACK A roughly built cottage

Page 21 **THE GECKO** There are many species of this Lizard in Australia, including the Zig Zig, Marbled, Leaf Tailed, Wood and House Gecko. The House Gecko can grow to 150mm. It is quite harmless and in tropical areas is welcomed as a house pet because it devours unwanted insects. It hides through the day, usually behind a picture or furniture.

GAME Slang for work.

Page 22 **THE KOOKABURRA** Also called the Laughing Jackass, it belongs to the Kingfisher family and has fascinated locals and visitors alike with its rollicking call that resembles human laughter. From earliest times it has been the drovers alarm clock as several will set up a hearty chorus at the first hint of daybreak. It grows to about 40 cm and is common throughout Australia.

Page 23 **THE WHITE COCKATOO** This large white parrot with bright yellow crest, grows to about 50 cm and is a common pet as it can be easily taught to imitate human speech. However because of its loud raucous screeching, it is not popular with neighbours. In the wild it flocks in large numbers and can do considerable damage to crops at harvest time.

Page 24 **BUNNY** A pet name for rabbit.

Page 25 **HARES AND RABBITS** While closely related species, they have distinctive differences. Rabbits are very social, while hares tend to be solitary. Hares are tall and slender, while rabbits tend to crouch or huddle. These animals are not native to Australia but they are as common as any local fauna. Introduced by the early European settlers, they have thrived and reached plague proportions. The Australian Government has an ongoing programme to control their numbers.

Page 26 **THE OWL** There are several species of this nocturnal feeder found in Australia. Its diet includes insects, mice, small birds and lizards. It grows to about 40 cm and is often found roosting in old barns and sheds.

Page 27 **THE PARROT** This general name covers a host of birds from tiny Budgerigars to Galahs, Kings, Rosellas and many more. Each variety has beautiful bright plumage. The Rainbow Lorikeet has become famous with tourists who love to feed them at Bird Sanctuaries, while Budgerigars are very popular as caged pets.

Page 28 **WOOLLY LAMB** It was truthfully said in years gone by, that Australia lived off the sheep's back. The great flocks of famous Merino sheep that covered vast areas of grasslands, produced the highest quality fleeces for export all over the world and gave rise to the name "The Land of the Golden Fleece". However in more recent years, artificial fibres have grown in popularity, reducing the demand for natural fibres such as wool.

Page 29 **TASSIE DEVIL** Their name makes them sound worse than they are, although they have never been in demand as house pets. These rather fierce looking residents of Tasmania, display a rather frightening arrray of sharp teeth in their oversize jaws. Their diet includes literally anything they can sink those teeth into, from cattle carcasses to grass. They are usually black with a white splash on the chest and lower back. The female will often carry up to three young clinging to her back. At feeding times there is usually a great deal of snapping and snarling and pushing, but serious wounds are seldom inflicted on fellow guests.

Page 30 **PINK AND GREY GALAH** This comical parrot grows to about 35 cm and is found in large numbers throughout Australia, especially in outback areas. Seen as a pest by crop farmers, it never the less endears itself to most people due to its comical behaviour. This includes hanging upside down from power lines during rain showers in order to get a good wash. Its often erratic flight gives the impression it is a stupid bird, resulting in the common term for a foolish person, "He's a real galah!"

THISTLE A wild plant with milky sap, bearing seeds relished by parrots.

Page 31 **TURTLES** They come in a range of types and sizes, from the small freshwater species found in coastal streams, to the large seagoing Loggerheads and Green Turtles. Some Australian beaches have become famous for turtle hatchings, none more so than Mon Repos near Bundaberg, South Queensland. Tourists flock there every year to observe this natural spectacle that takes place on certain nights when there is a full moon. The females swim ashore to lay their eggs in shallow depressions made in the sand, they then scrape sand over them before returning to sea. Their offspring are now on their own. About two months later the tiny hatchlings break out and begin the mad scramble toward the ocean, while an army of sea birds gorge themselves. Enough survive to keep the species going. The small fresh water turtles which can grow up to 30 cm are dwarfed by their sea going cousins that can grow to 1.5 meters.

DIN Noise   **BROOK** Creek

Page 32 **POSSUM** This Australian resident comes in several species and sizes. The two most common being the Ring-tail and the Brush-tail, but includes smaller species such as the Pigmy Glider and the Sugar Glider. The Brush-tail is probably the easiest to tame and will soon get accustomed to hand outs of fruit and other tasty morsels. Some years ago on a camper holiday in Tasmania, we had five large creamy coloured Brush tails in the van, quiet unafraid and scrambling over everything, to eat whatever was on offer.

Page 33 **TADPOLE** This middle stage between larvae and frog is spent in the water, where the tadpole breathes through fish-like gills. The tadpole must develop lungs before it can leave the water to live on land as a frog. This miraculous process takes place by design in just a few days and does not require millions of years.

Page 34 **NUMBAT** The Numbat is another ant-eating marsupial, but it does not have a pouch. It carries up to four young on its teats until they are old enough to be left in the burrow while mother forages outside. This animal is quite small, weighing less than half a kilogram. It has a striking coat of reddish brown with several white bands and large bushy tail. When standing upright it resembles the squirrel. The Numbat is just one more endangered species, and can now be found only in limited areas of South West Australia. Feral animals such as dogs and cats have reduced its number, and it is now illegal to take house pets into National Parks.

Page 35 **THE SWAGMAN** The Swagman (or Swaggie) became a common sight on Australian roads during the years of the Great Depression just prior to the Second World War. The expression to "hump one's bluey" or swag meant to walk, carrying one's bedroll and other belongings, and tramp the highways in search of work or the next feed. It has been recorded that hundreds of Australian men took up this nomadic existence, during those difficult years, often accompanied by a faithful dog.

DAMPER A bush bread baked in a pan over an open fire, consisting of self raising flour, salt and water.

BILLY Usually a large jam or fruit tin with a wire handle to boil water for tea. When the water is boiled, tea leaves were dropped in and the billy swung to settle the leaves.

Page 37 **FAIRY WREN** (Superb Fairy Wren) There are several species of this small bird about the size and shape of the Willy Wagtail. The above species has vivid blue plumage of various shades around the head and chest. Despite its small size it is not timid, but quite inquisitive.

FRILLED LIZARD This lizard is best known for its bright collar or frill which, when fully extended, gives this small lizard a threatening appearance. The frilly collar can range from bright orange to red. Like many lizards this one spends most of its time in trees seeking out insects to eat. If you surprise one on the ground it will likely run off upright on its back legs to scale the nearest tree. It is the reptile emblem of Australia.

BENT WING BAT This tiny member of the very extensive Bat family grows to about 115mm. It roosts communally, often in caves or disused mines in colonies up to several thousand. It sleeps during the day, venturing out in the cool of the evening to feed on insects.

Page 38 **QUAIL** This small chicken-like bird is found along the Australian coast, usually in open grasslands. The best opportunity to see them is when they cross the road or track and often with eight or ten chicks following. Their speckled plumage is brown to cream.

MALLEE FOWL This bird is found mainly across Southern Australia and has a similar nesting manner to the Brush Turkey. The male builds and maintains a large mound of sticks, earth and forest debris. When the female is ready to lay, he digs into the mound to create a brood chamber, then dutifully replaces the material to establish an incubator. He regularly checks the ground temperature and takes off, or piles on more material as the need may be, until the chicks hatch. This fowl grows to about 60 cm.

Page 39 **BUSH FLIES** The idea of tying several corks to a wide brimmed hat to keep flies off one's face seems to have originated with the Australian swaggie of bygone days. All flies can be a health hazard so it is wise to keep food and eating utensils covered.

Page 40 **TOAD** The most common species is the Cane Toad which proliferate in the vast cane fields of North Queensland, but have gradually spread into South Queensland and Northern New South Wales. The Toad was introduced from South America to control Cane Beetle which was attacking the sugarcane. While the female has a generally smooth skin, the male is covered with wart-like lumps which does detract from its natural beauty. The very sight of these creatures hopping across a lawn is enough to send the ladies scurrying for high ground. It is quite harmless to humans, but can poison water troughs and kill snakes or other predators that swallow them. Despite these negatives, there are some people who just dote on them, keeping them as pets.

Page 42 **FAT TOM** It is hoped that this rhyme will encourage children (and some adults) to exercise moderation.

Page 43 **BILLY BOCK** Children have a natural desire to share in all family activities, often copying adult behaviour. As with adults, things do not always go well, mistakes happen. Wise parents patiently teach and encourage, rather than constantly scold. What one of us does not blossom from a kind word, or a little encouragement.

Page 44 **HERBERT HATHAWAY AND BOBBY BOTTOMLY** It is hoped that these rhymes will encourage
45 little ones to always obey Mummy and Daddy.
46
47 **PEARLY WHITES** Teeth

CONCLUSION DO YOU NOT AGREE THAT THE COUNTLESS MARVELS IN THE NATURAL WORLD AROUND US, GIVE OVERWHELMING EVIDENCE OF BRILLIANT DESIGN BY A LOVING AND INTELLIGENT CREATOR?